MW00882430

THE CANE

THE CANE

Revised Edition

H. Lee Childress

Illustrations by Mary M. Smith

XULON PRESS

Xulon Press
2301 Lucien Way #415
Maitland, FL 32751
407.339.4217
www.xulonpress.com

© 2020 by H. Lee Childress

All rights reserved solely by the author. The author
guarantees all contents are original and do not
infringe upon the legal rights of any other person or
work. No part of this book may be reproduced in any
form without the permission of the author. The views
expressed in this book are not necessarily those of
the publisher.

Printed in the United States of America.

ISBN-13: 978-1-6312-9364-1

TABLE OF CONTENTS

Chapter 1

FRIENDS

IN A SMALL TOWN it would seem that everyone knows everybody and nobody has anything to hide. But, in this small town there seemed to be an exception, at least to the kids.

During the summer, life in a small town is lazy and filled with adventures that happen at a moments notice. On this particular hot and sunny day, several of the kids were bike riding down by the Methodist Church. The street is flat there, and large trees on both sides of the road, provide much needed shade on such a hot day.

Alice Jameson and her best friend Sara Pauls, were often found riding on this stretch of road, since school let out. Sara and Alice have been friends since preschool.

Sara's family lives just five houses down the street on the next block.

Today, a couple of their friends were there riding too. One was Billy Baxter, the show off, who always copied what Alice did and tried to do it better. Once Alice rode with no hands through a puddle of water, Billy did it the same way, but with his eyes closed.

Billy lives across the street from Alice. Whenever she and her friends are playing outside, he runs over to join in. He is very competitive and wants to be better than Alice at everything. Most of the time Alice doesn't mind him joining in, because she and Sara have so much fun teaming up against him.

Then there was Jenny Little. Jenny is two years younger than the others, at 8 years old, but she liked to hang around with the older girls. Alice complained to her mother once that at 10 years old, she was too old to hang out with babies like Jenny. Her mother told her that Jenny didn't have anyone to play with and that she should let her play with them. Alice didn't like it, but her mom made her promise not to be mean to Jenny.

Jenny's mom has been ill lately, so Jenny comes over a lot, now that it's summer. They live in the house around the corner. Alice remembered when Sara was sick, she and Jenny actually had a pretty good time playing together.

On this day the four were playing follow the leader. Sara was leading all the bikers up and down and around the road. Sara was followed by Jenny, Alice, and then of course Billy, who had to do everything better than Alice.

Chapter 2

THE CANE

A S THEY RODE DOWN the sidewalk, Sara noticed someone coming from the other direction. She turned to Alice and said, "Here comes the Cane!" "The Cane," Alice thoughvt nervously. The kids in the neighborhood called the old man who lived on the hill above the church "the Cane." Everybody knew he was mean because he never smiled at them the way other grownups do. He just grumbled and snarled. He would yell at the kids who cut across his yard to get to the corner store. Alice had even seen him swing his cane at a neighbor's dog that tried to sniff at him. All the kids were afraid of him.

He was an old man, probably 70 years old. His name was Mr. Smith. He rarely came down off the hill from his house. Whenever he did, he always had a black, silver tipped cane. It had a T shaped handle and a pointy silver tip on the end. The silver tip clicked on the sidewalk loudly, warning everyone that "the Cane" was near. That sound had frightened kids as long as Alice could remember. They stayed far away from him.

He was very thin with dark chocolate colored skin. His hair was gray on the sides of his head. None of them knew if the rest of his head was gray, because he never took off the old greasy ball cap. He bent over when he walked. His face was wrinkled and sagging. He never smiled. He just ambled down the sidewalk to the post office and then he would amble right back. His cane would click out every step. He always wore the same old denim jacket even when it was hot. Alice had always tried to steer clear of him. This time he was walking right toward them.

At the next driveway, Sara quickly turned off the sidewalk back into the street. Jenny followed and Alice was about to turn off the sidewalk at the same driveway as the others, until Billy blocked her path. To show off, Billy jumped off the sidewalk right beside Alice. Alice could not get off without hitting Billy and swerved back onto the sidewalk. Alice was so scared when she looked up and saw the Cane walking up in front of her. The clicking of the silver tip of his cane seemed to get louder and louder. She tried to swerve into the grass, but her front wheel hit a rock. Alice and her bike went flying. She landed on the ground with a thud. She hit her knee really hard and skinned up her elbows. Alice began to cry as she lay on the ground holding her knee to ease the pain.

Alice stopped crying when a gentle hand touched her shoulder and a calm voice asked if she were 'okay'. She thought it was Billy ready to apologize for causing her to wreck. She turned to see Mr. Smith's kindly old eyes looking at her. Frightened at first, she wondered how such kind eyes could belong to such a mean old man.

At that moment, the other kids were there to check on her and Billy didn't apologize or anything. He said, "I would'a jumped that rock!" It made Alice so mad! She was about to tell him a thing or two when she saw her bike. Her anger turned to sadness and she remembered the pain in her knee and began to sob again. The front wheel of her bike was bent all out of shape, the handle bars were crooked and she had a flat tire. She had forgotten the pain of her knee and elbows because she had been so mad at Billy. Now seeing her bike all broken she could not stop crying.

Mr. Smith helped her up and said, "How about you let me fix your bike, since I was in your way on the sidewalk." Alice stopped crying when she heard his offer to fix her bike. She looked into those kindly old eyes as she wiped her tears. He said, "You come by my house tomorrow afternoon and I will have it ready for you. You scoot on home now and let your mother look at those scrapes, but don't forget to pick up your bike tomorrow."

Alice watched as the old man dragged her bike up the hill toward his house. Alice hobbled home with the help of Sara and Jenny. Billy road circles around them, all the way to Alice's driveway. His last words were, "I would've jumped clear over that rock," and then he sped off to his house.

Chapter 3

HISTORY LESSON

ALICE'S MOM SHEILA WASHED her scrapes and put medicine and a bandage on each one. The medicine hurt almost as much as the bike wreck. Alice let out a squeal each time her mother applied the medicine. Her mom blew gently on the sore area after putting on the medicine, the cool air always made it feel better.

Alice's mom asked her what happened to her bike. Alice told her what had happened with "the Cane uh, Mr. Smith." and how nice he was to her and not mean at all. Her mother scolded her about judging people. Alice told her the things that she had seen and the things the other kids talked about.

"He said he would fix my bike, but I think he may just keep it." Her mother said, "Alice, if Mr. Smith says he will have your bike fixed by tomorrow, it will be, and we are going together to get it."

It turns out that Alice's mom knew Mr. Smith as a kind man when she was a little girl. "Let me tell you something about Mr. Henry Thadeus Smith. Mr. Smith used to own the local garage in town. He could fix anything. He fixed cars, bikes, fans and almost anything anyone in town brought to his garage. He also gave us kids free sodas when we had to wait for him to repair our bikes."

"Why doesn't he still own a garage and why does he always look so shabby?" asked Alice.

"Well, that's another story. When Mr. Smith bought the garage, he had very little money and was planning to marry. He worked very hard and saved all he could. After a few months his business began to make money."

Alice's mom finished wrapping her scrape with gauze and kissed her elbow. She always did that after mending Alice's scrapes and bruises. She gently pulled Alice into her lap so as not to bump her hurting elbows or knee.

Alice's mom looked up at the ceiling as if looking back into the past and began her story about Mr. Smith. As she stroked Alice's hair, she told how Mr. Smith's wedding was the talk of the town. Everyone was so happy for them. She told Alice how hard Mr. Smith and his wife worked in that garage late into the night, working toward a dream.

"Mr. and Mrs. Smith soon opened another garage in the next town. In five years, they had four garages across the county. As the money started rolling in, they decided they were ready to start a family." Alice's mom tapped Alice's nose with her finger and winked at her. "They couldn't have been happier together expecting to have their first child."

Everything then seemed to change. Alice's mom hugged her tight and kissed her cheek. Alice looked at her mom and asked, "What's wrong mommy?" After a deep sigh, Alice's mom continued the story.

"Well, Mr. Smith saw an opportunity to buy three more garages in the state capital. They would make a lot of money for his family. The deal went through and he was right, the three garages made lots of money for Mr. and Mrs. Smith and their expected child."

"They now had workers to run the shops for them which gave them some free time together. They used the free time away from the garage to shop for baby things and long walks at the park. Then one day, Mrs. Smith collapsed while at the grocery store, and was rushed to the hospital. Mr. Smith was out of town checking on a problem at one of his garages. When Mr. Smith arrived at the hospital the first person he met at the door was Reverend Colstern. Just by the look in Rev. Colstern's eyes he could tell something was wrong."

By this time Alice's father had sat down beside them, to listen to the story and to see if Alice was okay. He gently touched the scrapes on Alice's knee. Alice quickly pulled her knee away and gave her dad a glare that voiced her displeasure. Alice's mom smiled at the two of them and asked, "Can I finish my story now?" Dad gave mom a nod to go ahead.

"Mrs. Smith and their expected child had both died in the operating room, due to problems of the birth. What Mr. Smith thought was going to be the happiest day of his life, the birth of his first child, turned out to be his worst."

"Oh mommy, that is so sad," said Alice, as a tear rolled down her cheek. Alice's father agreed and wiped away her tear with a swipe of his thumb on her cheek. "Is that why he is so mad about everything?" asked Alice.

"Well, he went away for quite a while. When he returned, he stayed to himself because he didn't want to talk about his pain." Alice's mom leaned back and looked Alice squarely in the eye and said, "Alice, you can't judge people without getting to know something about them first."

At that moment, Alice remembered Mr. Smith's kindly old eyes and his gentle touch. She thought to herself, maybe he wasn't mean at all, maybe he just needed a friend. That night, Alice decided that she had to go pick up her bike with her mother tomorrow. She wanted to see for herself, if there was a nice man inside the mean person she knew only as "the Cane."

Chapter 4

FACE TO FACE

THE NEXT MORNING ALICE looked and sounded like a very old lady, instead of a ten-year old full of energy. Her elbows and her knee were so sore when she woke up. She moaned and groaned with every movement. It took her nearly 30 minutes to get dressed. She hobbled down to meet her mom and dad in the kitchen for breakfast. Today, even chewing seemed to make her sores throb. Alice caught her dad trying to cover up his smile at her obvious discomfort. He apologized, but burst out laughing saying, "I'm sorry sweetie, but you're moving around like grampa!" Alice wanted to pinch him, but all she could do was laugh.

As the morning wore on, she began to move better and better. Her mom said they would go to pick up her bike after lunch, to give Mr. Smith time to fix it. Alice decided to call Sara to see if she could go with her. Sara had always thought Mr. Smith was creepy and mean. When Alice talked to Sara about going, Sara sounded panicky and scared. She didn't want to go, but when Alice told her that her mother was going with them, she agreed to go. Sara still wasn't sure about Mr. Smith though.

Just after lunch, Alice's mom grabbed her purse and told Alice to meet her on the porch. It was finally time to go. Alice was trying to slip her shoes on when she bumped her elbow on the corner of the chair. She was quickly reminded that she was not totally healed yet. The pain shot up her arm and she nearly screamed. She stood there breathing deeply until the pain slowly went away. Alice joined her mom on the porch to walk to Mr. Smith's house. They picked up Sara on the way. She was waiting in her front yard with her bike, so she and Alice could ride their bikes home, if Mr. Smith really fixed it.

On the way Alice and Sara began retelling all the stories they had heard about "the Cane." Sara said, "Duane Bland said he saw Mr. Smith beating someone with his cane in his garage one time!"

Alice's mom looked at Sara and said, "Sara if that were true, Mr. Smith would have been arrested. Don't believe everything Duane Bland says. Isn't he the one that Mr. Augustine caught stealing his fishing pole last week?" Alice and Sara nodded, as they agreed Duane probably wasn't the most dependable person to believe.

"What about the time he took the boys' baseball that went into his yard by accident?" said Alice. "When Billy went in to get it Mr. Smith raised his cane and yelled at him. That's why we started calling him 'the Cane.'" Alice said matter-of-factly.

"I remember talking to Mrs. Baxter about that," replied Mrs. Jameson. "Billy trampled right through Mr. Smith's tomatoes and ruined his plants. He told Mrs. Baxter that Billy could come and get the ball, when he apologized. Billy was too scared to go back, so he never got the ball."

As the three approached Mr. Smith's house, he wasn't sitting in his customary place on the front porch. Sara didn't mind that. As a matter of fact, she was hoping he wasn't home at all. When they got closer, they heard whistling coming from the back of the house. Alice's mom figured he must be working in his garage in the back. The whistling sounded very happy and pleasant. Alice thought, This couldn't be "the Cane."

When Alice's mom called out his name, Mr. Smith opened the door and greeted them. He said, "Sheila Prost, is that you?"

"It's me Mr. Smith," Alice's mom replied, "but its Jameson now." "This is my daughter Alice and her friend Sara."

"The resemblance is uncanny. I should have known," replied Mr. Smith. "I haven't stopped to help anyone in years, but there was something about this little girl. I hope you didn't mind me taking the bike yesterday," Mr. Smith said.

"No Sir! As a matter of fact, I told her you were a man of your word."

"I'll bet you didn't know that your mother used to bring her bike to me when it needed fixing did you?" he asked Alice. Alice shook her head no. "Your mother was such a sweet young lady. My wife and I thought so much of her that we…that we…"

"Mr. Smith are you alright?" Alice's mom asked as she gently touched his arm. He looked up at her and said, "We hoped our daughter would be as sweet and kind as you." Alice's mom hugged Mr. Smith and said, "I'm sure she would have been a sweet girl with parents as good and kind as the two of you."

Alice and Sara didn't know what to think. They both looked at each other with eyebrows raised, not knowing what to make of Mr. Smith.

Just then Mr. Smith stiffened and turned to the girls and said, "Enough of this! Lets' take a look at that bike." He looked at Alice with a smile and removed the white sheet that was covering her bicycle. Alice's eyes were wide with astonishment. She could not believe it. Her old bike looked brand new. Without thinking, Alice was hugging Mr. Smith, saying thank you, thank you!

Not only had Mr. Smith repaired the crooked handle bars and fixed the flat tire, he had painted it and added some reflectors. Alice's bike was better than new. She asked her mom, "Can I ride it now?"

Her mom looked at Mr. Smith who nodded and then said, "Yes."

Sara and Alice laughed and giggled as they rode circles in the driveway. He told Alice's mom that he had lots of leftover bicycle parts in his garage. The girls laughter made Mr. Smith smile. His smile never left, even as Alice's mom thanked him and said goodbye.

As they neared the end of the drive, Alice turned and rode back to Mr. Smith's garage. He was just closing the garage door when he was surprised by Alice's arms wrapped around his waist. Alice said, "Thank you Mr. Smith, and I'm sorry for all the things I thought about you before."

Mr. Smith hugged her back and said, "I probably deserved it, because I haven't been very nice lately."

Looking at Alice with those kindly old eyes Mr. Smith said, "Thank you, for helping me find myself again. Now you run along and enjoy that bike." Alice did exactly that. Sara and Alice never thought of Mr. Smith the same after that day. They never called him "the Cane" again.

Chapter 5

FRIENDSHIP GROWS

FOR THE NEXT FEW years Mr. Smith and Alice's relationship grew. Mr. Smith became like a grandfather to Alice. He attended her soccer games and was always invited to family gatherings at the Jameson home. Alice would stop by often after school to talk with Mr. Smith about her day. He always gave her good advice. Mr. Smith would tell Alice about the adventures of his youth. Alice and Mr. Smith would sit and rock on his porch for hours. Because of Alice and Sara, most of the kids in the neighborhood stopped calling Mr. Smith, "the Cane." It would take a while longer for Billy.

Mr. Smith was the first person Alice called, when she found out the grade on her science project in Jr. High school. They had spent a lot of time working on it together. She made an 'A'. Mr. Smith beamed with pride. Alice also used Mr. Smith's knowledge of World War II during her history class project. He had an actual helmet and uniform that Alice was able to use in her presentation. The other kids really liked all the pictures he had given her as well.

Alice helped Mr. Smith too. Mr. Smith wanted to plant a garden in his yard to grow flowers that his wife had really liked. Alice came by every day after school for a whole week, to help him dig and plant. The garden made Mr. Smith's yard look so inviting and friendly that many neighbors would stop to admire the colorful garden. Before, most of the neighbors tried to avoid looking toward his house at all.

For Christmas in her sophomore year, Alice used money from her weekend job at the corner store to buy Mr. Smith a new cane. It was brown with a rounded handle and a soft rubber stopper on the tip. Alice said the stopper was the most important part. It would stop the clicking on the sidewalk that gave Mr. Smith his previous nickname. Mr. Smith laughed with delight.

For Halloween that next year, Alice was on the dance committee for the high school Halloween dance. Mr. Smith, using scrap parts from his garage, built a mummy that sat up when people walked by. It was a big hit sitting at the entrance to the dance. Sara screamed so loud when it sat up next to her, that the principal came running out to see what was wrong. Alice was working the controls and fell over laughing at Sara. Sara wasn't too happy about it, but said she would forgive her, if she let her scare somebody too!

Chapter 6

PART OF THE FAMILY

MR. SMITH AND ALICE stayed close throughout her high school years. They didn't spend quite so much time together as they had during her early teens. Alice had a few more things on her mind now, including ball games, pep rallies, a part time job, and most of all boys. She did make sure to drop in on Mr. Smith one or two times a week though. Mr. Smith was not as active as he had been a few years ago. He didn't walk to the store everyday like he used to.

However, Mr. Smith did, make a little time for Billy Baxter. Last year, Billy's old car stopped right outside Mr. Smith's gate and he couldn't get it going. Mr. Smith said, "Push into my yard, and we'll see if we can get it working. They worked on it together. Mr. Smith did own several garages, and Billy wanted to be an auto mechanic. Billy was finally able to see that Mr. Smith wasn't so bad. He too stopped calling him "the Cane." Billy would stop by every couple of months or so, just to show Mr. Smith what new things he had done to his car.

Just before Mr. Smith's 81st birthday, Alice walked with him to the doctor's office on her way to work. Mr. Smith uses the same doctors' office as Alice, but he saw Dr. Robinson instead of Alice's doctor, Dr. Miller. He had said he wanted to get a checkup and that nothing was wrong. She didn't think anything of it, and he didn't mention the checkup when she stopped by later that week.

Alice's mom offered to have a birthday party for Mr. Smith at their house, as they had done the year before on his 80th birthday. It was so fun last year to see Mr. Smith smiling and joking with old friends and enjoying himself. She told Alice that Mr. Smith had declined the party, because he wasn't feeling very well at the moment. Alice bought a card and baked him some cupcakes. He loved chocolate cupcakes. She wanted to check on him, as well as wish him a Happy Birthday.

Alice found Mr. Smith in bed when she arrived. She asked, "What's wrong Mr. Smith? Do you have a spring cold?" Mr. Smith struggled to smile and replied, "I'm just a little under the weather." "Well, I brought you some cupcakes and a birthday card," said Alice, as she handed Mr. Smith the card. As Mr. Smith read the card his eyes started to well up with tears. Alice smiled and handed him a tissue from the box by the bed. Mr. Smith held Alice's hand for a moment and said, "Thank you Alice, you don't know how much your friendship has meant to me. I'll be better in a couple of days and I will need your help with something."

"Well, just give me a call when you need me." Alice said, as she walked out the door. As she left the yard, Alice couldn't help but wonder why Mr. Smith had become so emotional.

Two days later was Friday, and Alice was headed for a three day spring break trip with friends to Lake Teranu. She made sure all of her chores and packing were done. Sara was picking her up in her father's station wagon at one o'clock. Alice didn't want to miss this trip. Sara and two other girl friends from school, Chelsea Fields and Jordan Childers, had rented a cabin. They had all pooled their money from their after school jobs.

The four had become friends during PE in 9th grade. Billy had convinced a couple of his friends to ambush Alice and Sara during a dodgeball game. Chelsea and Jordan are very athletic and jumped in to save them. They pelted Billy and his buddies until they surrendered. The four have been friends ever since.

Several of the boys from school were going to the lake to ski this weekend as well. One of them was Billy Baxter, who turned out not to be such a jerk after all. Sara was shy about admitting it, because of how he used to be, but she kind of liked Billy Baxter now. Alice liked, really liked, Billy's new friend Evan. Evan had only moved here from up state six months ago. Alice thought he was the sweetest, most handsome boy she had ever met. They had two classes together and he made it hard for Alice to concentrate sometimes.

When Mr. Smith called at 11:00 to ask if Alice would drive him downtown, she felt a little panicky. "Oh no, not now" she thought. She didn't want to be late, but she had promised him she would help him. She half-heartedly agreed and rushed to his house, so she could get whatever it was over with. Mr. Smith told Alice how much better he felt as they drove in his old car, a 1969 four door Oldsmobile. Mr. Smith drove like the old man he was, very slow. Alice kept looking at her watch.

Alice was surprised when Mr. Smith pulled into the Ford Auto Dealership. She asked kind of surprised, "Mr. Smith, are you getting a new car?" He said, "Yep, I think it's about time to upgrade." They looked at practical cars that he could haul his groceries in. They looked at tiny sports cars that Mr. Smith said, "might make me drive faster," with a laugh. Just as Alice looked at her watch for the 10th time, he said, "Alice, if you were going to get a new car which one would you choose?"

Alice looked at Mr. Smith and said, "Now you know I am a little younger than you and I am a girl." Alice turned immediately and pointed to a cute, sporty, yellow car on the front row. Mr. Smith said, "That is a nice, but can you see me in that bright colored car going down to the parts store?" They both laughed. "But, for you Mr.

Smith, I think the silver midsize is the way to go." Mr. Smith agreed and told the salesman to hold the car, he would be back to talk to him about the purchase.

Knowing that Alice had to leave soon, he persuaded her to drive so they would not be late. That old Oldsmobile had probably not gone that fast in long time. They made it just in time. Sara, Jordan and Chelsea had just pulled into the driveway. Alice waved goodbye to Mr. Smith and loaded her things into Sara's father's station wagon. Off they went for three days of water skiing and fun.

Chapter 7

CALIFORNIA COUSINS

ALICE AND HER FRIENDS had a blast at the lake. It was their last high school fling before graduation. Alice got to know Evan Johnson much better. She found out he was as juvenile as the rest of the boys that she knew. He made fun of Alice when she fell off the rope swing and basically ignored her when the other guys were around. She still thought he was cute though. Sara and Billy did become an item that weekend and began dating. Alice thought Jordan and Josh Lyon would make a cute couple, but Jordan thought Josh was weird. Besides, Jordan had her eye on Todd Burks a star on the football team.

When Alice got home that Tuesday, she was so tired that she slept all day. That night she told her mom and dad all about the trip. She then spent the rest of the night talking on the phone to Sara and Chelsea about all that happened at the lake. They laughed and screamed playfully as they relived every moment.

The next day Alice got up early to take a walk and stop by to see Mr. Smith. She wanted to see if he actually bought the car she had recommended. Alice's mom said, "Oh, honey I forgot to tell you that Mr. Smith called while you were away. He was going to visit relatives in California. He was going to drive that new car that you chose for him and see the country. He wants you to pick up his mail and water his plants while he's gone."

A smile came across Alice's face for two reasons. Mr. Smith had really taken her advice on the car. She was also happy that he was reconnecting with his relatives after all these years. "How long will he be gone?" asked Alice. "He wasn't sure, answered her mom, but he said he would definitely be back to see you graduate." Graduation was a little over a month away.

Alice went to Mr. Smith's house to water the flowers and pick up the mail. She did a little weeding in the flower garden they had planted together years ago. Sometimes one of her friends would come along to help out. As she wiped her forehead and looked back at the porch almost expecting to see him, her mind began to wonder.

Why had Mr. Smith taken this trip all of a sudden? He had never even mentioned any relatives to her. Was something wrong that Mr. Smith wasn't telling her? But, why buy a new car if there was something wrong? It was a long drive to California! Would he be okay?

She quizzed her parents when she got home, but they were no help. They didn't know anything about his family.

About two weeks later as Alice and Jordan were watering the plants at Mr. Smith's. Jordan said, "If I had a little shovel, I could work this area better." Alice was checking around the garage to see if there might be one lying around, when she peeked in the window. She noticed something in the locked garage. She couldn't see it very well, because the blinds were pulled shut. Through a crack she could see a car covered with a tarp inside. Alice smiled and said to herself, "That old faker, he couldn't get rid of that old Oldsmobile after all. Jordan, I can't find a shovel. Let me get the mail and then we can leave."

SMITH, H.T.

The mail didn't help Alice's suspicions that something was wrong. Mr. Smith was receiving mail from the hospital and Dr. Robinson's office about once a week. Maybe she could ask Dr. Robinson what was going on. "No, a doctor can't tell you about another patient," responded Jordan. "I learned that the first day, when I worked as the file clerk after school at the hospital last summer."

"I'll just have to wait till he gets back then," said Alice.

A little over two weeks after he left, Mr. Smith called to let Alice and the Jameson's know that he had made it to California. Alice's dad said, "Well, hello Mr. Smith, we were beginning to worry about you." Alice was at his shoulder, waving for the phone before he could finish the sentence. Alice's dad said, "I think there is someone here who really wants to talk to you, we're glad you're okay." Alice almost ripped the phone from his hands, but kissed his cheek as an apology.

Mr. Smith asked Alice about her trip and school. Mr. Smith seemed very interested in "this Evan character" as he called him. Alice asked about his trip and relatives. Mr. Smith told her he had made several overnight stops so he wouldn't get too tired. He also made a few side trips. He spent two days at the Grand Canyon and another couple of days, fishing at a mountain lake. He didn't seem to want to talk about his relatives at all, so Alice didn't push it. He must not like them she thought.

Mr. Smith assured Alice that he had just forgotten to pay the doctor and hospital bill before he left and that everything was alright. Mr. Smith encouraged Alice to give Evan another chance, but away from his buddies this time, to see what he is really like. Alice agreed, and told Mr. Smith that she was taking very good care of their garden. They talked for almost an hour. Mr. Smith said he had better go, so he can get a bite to eat before bedtime. He promised to call her first thing when he returned. Alice smiled as she put down the phone. She was happy he was okay. Mr. Smith seemed like his old self.

Chapter 8

Night on the Town

MR. SMITH RETURNED EXACTLY one week before Alice's graduation. Alice was nervous that he would not make it back in time. She really wanted him to be there, because he had been such a big part of her high school years. Alice had received an academic scholarship offer, from State University in Laurel City, about 150 miles away. She hadn't told Mr. Smith yet, because she wanted to tell him in person.

When she went to visit him the next day, he looked very tired, and it worried Alice. He reminded Alice of how she felt after just three days at the lake. Alice shook her head and said, "Ok, I remember. I'll let you rest a while, but tomorrow you are going to have to take me riding in your new car." He agreed.

The next day after school Alice and Mr. Smith went to dinner in his new car. He was feeling much better and they had a great time. They saw Sara and Billy, who were getting quite serious about each other, at the local restaurant. They were sharing a pizza. Mr. Smith took her to play miniature golf and she won! As they left the miniature golf course Alice broke the news that she would be going to State University next year on an academic scholarship. Mr. Smith was very pleased and said, "This calls for ice cream!" Alice recommended they go to Brenda's Ice Cream shop, even though there were places to get ice cream closer. At Brenda's, Alice introduced Mr. Smith to Evan Johnson. Mr. Smith could see now it was not by chance she had chosen this place. Alice knew Evan would be working.

Mr. Smith slowly spooned his ice cream as he watched the two young people coyly chat with one another. Alice could see now that Mr. Smith was right, Evan was as charming as ever, now that he was away from his buddies. He even paid for their ice cream, and asked if he and Alice could play miniature golf together sometime. Alice was so smitten with Evan, she said, "Sure, anytime, bye!" as she walked out the gate to leave.

She had totally forgotten about Mr. Smith sitting at the table! Embarrassed, she smiled, walked back in and said, "Well, aah, Mr. Smith, I guess we had better go." Mr. Smith laughed and shook Evan's hand, thanking him for the ice cream. Alice rushed to get him out before Mr. Smith could say something to embarrass her even more.

Chapter 9

GRADUATION DAY

THE DAY OF ALICE'S graduation was a hectic one. Hair, makeup, shoes and dress all had to be checked and done. Alice had volunteered to bring cookies for the graduation party after. She was going to bake them herself. She also had to remember to buy film for her camera. She wanted pictures to record the events of the night. The seniors were allowed to miss school that day to prepare for the ceremony that night.

Alice took the last batch of cookies out of the oven and set them aside to cool. She decided to run to the camera shop with Billy and Sara, to get the film and pick up her dress. As Alice was leaving the camera shop, she stopped. She saw Dr. Robinson down the block talking with Mr. Smith, as if he was consoling him. He had his hand on Mr. Smith's shoulder while Mr. Smith hung his head. Sara and Billy were yelling at her to hurry up. She hopped in the car with the intention of asking Mr. Smith about it later at the graduation ceremony.

That night was one to remember. The city's largest graduating class ever was saying farewell to high school. All the parents and friends were there, dressed in their best Sunday clothes. The minister opened the proceedings with a prayer. Then the national anthem was sung by Pamela Miller, accompanied by the school band. Pamela was the only choir member to make All State this year, she had a beautiful voice. She was also, the first to be embarrassed by family members in the audience. Her uncle yelled out, "Atta girl Pammy!" as she finished singing.

As Alice and the other graduates marched in, Alice strained to see where her parents were sitting. The stands were packed and cameras were flashing everywhere. She didn't spot them until she saw a cane sticking out above all the waving hands. It was Mr. Smith. Alice smiled and gave a very quick wave. Mr. Middleton, the principal, had warned them not to make a commotion during the ceremony.

The speaker that night was a former student from the high school that had made a name for herself in business. Everyone knew Sharon Blain. She was the most notable success story to graduate from this school. She went into real estate soon after high school and now owns the largest real estate firm in the region. She talked to the graduates about having dreams and the determination to turn those dreams into reality. She had made her fortune by the time she was 35 years old and donated lots of money to area charities and to the school.

She spoke so kindly about Mrs. Fincher, whom she credited with teaching her to excel in algebra. The graduates started to snicker because they didn't realize Mrs. Fincher was that old.

Miss Blain received a huge ovation at the end of her speech. Alice took her words to heart, because she too dreamed of being successful. She wasn't sure what she was going to do, but she hoped her first year at college would help her decide.

It was now time for the graduates to receive their diplomas and walk across the podium. Alice was so excited. She stood and turned to follow the people in line and noticed Evan giving her the thumbs up sign. As Alice got closer to the stage, she began remembering all the good times she and her classmates had shared throughout their years here. She never thought she would miss her high school days this much. She began to look at all the faces and wondered what each would do after graduation. Kristy will marry Paul and live here in town the rest of their lives. Greg will be the one to go off to a big city and be very successful, and …, "Alice Jameson", the announcer said.

Alice tried to look calm as she strolled across the stage, only to stumble just as she reached out to shake the principal's hand. She was sure that she heard Sara's laughter as she regained control and adjusted her cap. She was embarrassed, but smiled and shook the principal's hand while receiving her diploma in the other hand. Pamela's Uncle yelled, "Atta girl Alice!" Alice could only smile and wave as she moved her tassel over to show she was a graduate.

When she left the stage, her parents were at the bottom ready to take her picture. She stood proudly holding her diploma. She was now officially a graduate. She marched back to her seat, without stumbling too.

After the final person received their diploma the principal said, "It is my pleasure to present to you, this year's Jefferson High School graduates!" There was howling, whistling, cheering and clapping from all over. The graduates threw their caps into the air as is tradition at graduation.

Alice searched the crowd and found her parents and Mr. Smith, and more pictures were taken. Sara and Chelsea came running up a few minutes later ready to go to the graduation dance. Alice hugged her parents and told them not to forget she needed to borrow the car tomorrow. She and the girls were going to drive to Laurel City to look around the campus. The Jamesons both nodded approvingly and then looked at Mr. Smith and smiled.

Alice gave Mr. Smith a big hug. He told her how proud he was of her. He asked her to stop by his house before leaving town tomorrow so he could give her his graduation gift. She agreed, and then arm in arm the girls skipped to the parking lot and off for a night of dancing.

Chapter 10

SURPRISE, SURPRISE!

THE NEXT DAY ALICE was awakened early by a phone call from Jordan. Jordan said she couldn't sleep all night long, thinking about Alice and Evan. Evan and Alice were together all night, dancing, walking, talking and arm in arm. Jordan wanted to hear all the details. Alice said, "I'll tell you all about it on the way to Laurel City, let me get up and get ready. Call the others and tell them to be ready. I'll be by to pick you guys up in an hour."

Alice showered quickly, hurriedly brushed her hair and teeth. Her dad reminded her that she had to stop by Mr. Smith's. "Okay", she replied as she pulled on a pair of jeans and a t-shirt. Her dad reminded her two more times while she quickly ate a doughnut and drank her juice, that she had promised to stop by Mr. Smith's before she left. She grabbed her keys and hopped into her dad's car with a bag of chips and a soda.

Finally, Alice said, "Dad alright I promise I will stop by Mr. Smith's before I leave!" She wondered why her dad was so worried about it. He was acting kind of strange. Alice decided to pick up the others on the way to Mr. Smith's. That way they could leave as soon as she picked up her graduation gift.

When the girls arrived at Mr. Smith's he was just saying goodbye to the minister. Alice got that strange feeling again that something was wrong. She never did get a chance to ask him about it. Mr. Smith looked tired, but happy to see Alice. She let the others wait in the car while she ran up to get her gift. "Well, Mr. Smith, here I am."

"Thank you for coming Alice. I wanted to give you your graduation present away from the crowd last night."

Alice said, "Mr. Smith, having you there last night meant so much to me. That was present enough. I know you haven't been feeling well."

"You know me very well child," he replied. "I am not well, but I would not have missed your graduation for anything."

They walked around to the garage and Alice helped Mr. Smith as he struggled with the door. Alice said, "I thought you were going to get rid of that old Oldsmobile," as she pointed to the car under the tarp. "I saw it still here when I came by to water the flowers."

Mr. Smith made a painful attempt to smile then said, "Do you remember when we went to pick out my new car?" Alice nodded. "Well, I also picked out one for you." He pulled the tarp back to reveal the bright yellow sports car that Alice liked from car lot.

Alice couldn't breathe for a few seconds. She was so surprised. "Mr. Smith no.., you shouldn't have."

"I talked it over with your parents weeks ago and they said it was alright if I did this." Alice knew they were acting a little strange every time she mentioned having a car.

He handed Alice the keys and she hugged his neck and squealed with glee. "Take her for a drive around the block. Lets' see how you look in it."

Alice got in and started the car, all the while saying, "Thank you, thank you, thank you!" She pulled out of the garage and the bright yellow car seemed to light up in the sunlight. Alice honked at her friends who didn't know what to think of her zooming past them in another car.

After the trip around the block, Alice pulled up next to her friends and said, "Hop in girls, lets' go for a ride!" Her friends screamed as they piled their gear into her new car. They could not believe it! "Mr. Smith said, "Your dad will pick up the other car later today."

They all waved as they drove down the street. Alice stopped suddenly, backed up and ran back to Mr. Smith standing in his yard. She gave him a big long hug. He whispered in her ear, "You are the daughter I always wanted. I love you as my own."

Alice, now in tears, looked into those same kindly old eyes she had seen as a little girl. She hugged him and said, "Thank you Mr. Smith." In the mirror as they drove away, she could see Mr. Smith standing in his driveway, waving goodbye.

Chapter 11

FAREWELL

THE GIRLS COULD NOT believe Mr. Smith had bought Alice a new car. Sara was wondering why didn't she hang out with Mr. Smith more, maybe she would have a car too. For the next 50 miles they played with every gadget and button the car had. They turned the music up loud and sang. They took turns driving, stopping at every rest stop along the way to switch drivers. It drove like a dream, nothing like her dad's old car.

Finally, they reached the State University campus. At the Student Union, they picked up a map of the campus. They walked around to get acquainted with the set up. They watched some of the football team going through drills on the football field. They even pretended to faint over the muscular athletes as they ran by. After an hour of touring the area, they stopped to get a bite to eat.

All the girls noticed that Alice seemed lost in thought. She was fairly quiet as they ate and talked about all the campus had to offer. Even the mention of the football guys didn't break her silence.

Sara finally said, "Alice what's wrong? You seem a million miles away." She said, "Guys, I should have talked to Mr. Smith about the doctor thing. I am just having this strange feeling." Chelsea wanted to go to that shopping mall they had heard about. Maybe it would get Alice's mind off things. "I've got a bad feeling, I think we need to go home," said Alice. The girls didn't want to go home yet. They wanted to hang out in the city a little longer.

They convinced Alice to call home to make sure everything was okay. They hoped that then she would get back to normal and they could stay. She agreed and called her mom. Her mom was glad that she called. "Oh, Alice, thank God you called." Mr. Smith was taken to the hospital about two hours after you left. The doctors did everything they could but …" "Oh no, mom," Alice replied with tears welling up in her eyes, "Is he…?"

"Yes dear, he died just a little while ago." Alice's tears fell like rain and she dropped the phone, sobbing as she knelt to the ground. The other girls rushed in to console her, wondering what had happened.

Sara picked up the phone to find out what happened. She told Alice's mom that they would start home immediately.

Chelsea drove all the way home. It was a quiet ride. Alice just stared out the window at the clouds, with her head on Sara's shoulder. She thought back to the first time she and Sara met Mr. Smith face to face. Alice thought about all the good times she and Mr. Smith had shared. She looked around the new car he had purchased for her. She began to chuckle and looked up at Sara saying, "the Cane' was a scary man when we were kids, wasn't he?"

"Remember how we met?" replied Sara. They both laughed as they remembered the bike wreck way back then. Alice pulled up her sleeve to show her elbow and said, "I still have the scars to prove it."

A week later, Alice and her parents attended Mr. Smith's funeral. It was a beautiful, but sad occasion. Alice and Chelsea had decorated the church with flowers from his garden. There was no family there for Mr. Smith, but many of the towns people he had befriended since he and Alice met, were there . Alice thought it was a shame, that none of the family that he had visited last month, was able to attend. She found out why later.

Alice stayed behind after the service to say goodbye to Mr. Smith in private. As she left, she saw her bright yellow car that Mr. Smith had given her. Alice smiled, knowing that every time she looked at that car she would be reminded of Mr. Smith.

A lawyer introduced himself to the Jamesons. He gave Alice's parents a letter to read. He asked them to be at the reading of Mr. Smith's Will the next afternoon.

Chapter 12

LAST WILL AND TESTAMENT

THE LAWYER BEGAN, "SINCE Mr. Smith had no family, his wish was to leave his Earthly belongings to you gathered here today. "Mr. Smith had no family? What about last month when he went to California to visit relatives?" Alice asked. The lawyer shook his head and said, "Mr. Smith went to California for treatment for his heart condition, from a specialist. He didn't want anyone to treat him with pity so he kept it a secret. He said the people in this room were his family, and his Will, which I will read now proves that."

Those present at the reading of his Will were: Mr. Campano, the owner of the grocery store Mr. Smith visited. Rev. Buchanan, the new minister at the church. Billy Baxter, Mr. Thompson the mayor, Dr. Robinson, who had diagnosed Mr. Smith's heart condition, Alice and her mom and dad. The lawyer then began to read.

I, Henry Thadeous Smith being of sound mind, hereby bequeath the following. To Mr. Campano I leave two round trip tickets to Italy for he and his lovely wife, along with 10,000 dollars cash. You were so kind to me and I enjoyed our talks about your homeland.

To Rev. Buchanan, I leave 200,000 dollars to finish the new addition on the church property. In my last days you gave me strength and helped me regain my faith.

To Billy Baxter, I leave all the tools in my home garage. I have also paid the tuition for you to attend the community technical college you dreamed of going to. I also leave you this worn old baseball. Good luck Billy, you will be a great mechanic.

To the Mayor of this city, I leave my home and the twelve acres it sits on. As we discussed, it is for the construction of a park for the younger children of the city. Another 400,000 dollars goes to the city for the park equipment and court construction. There is one stipulation. The park cannot be named for me. I was not a friendly person for the majority of my life. I do not want kids playing at a park with my name on it.

To Dr. Robinson, thank you for your care and thoughtfulness during my illness. As we talked over the last six months you mentioned needing a larger building to better serve your patients. I leave you the building downtown that you have been attempting to get a loan to buy. You are a good man and the people of this city need you. The building has been purchased for 300,000 thousand dollars. The lawyer handed Dr. Robinson the deed to the property.

Everyone was very happy and grateful for the gifts Mr. Smith had left them. None really knew he had that kind of money. Alice didn't think he had the money to afford her car, much less all of this. The lawyer then excused everyone from the room except Alice's family at Mr. Smith's request.

The lawyer closed the door and read. To the Jameson family, I leave the bulk of my estate. After the deduction of the other gifts, the lawyer paused…, that comes to 4.6 million dollars. Everyone's eyes were as big as saucers as they looked at each other.

The lawyer continued reading. I sold all seven of my repair shops to a large company wanting to expand in this area, a few years after my wife and child died. I didn't have anything or anyone else to spend the money on, so I invested it. The investments did very, very well.

As you have found out by now, I don't have family in California. You befriended me and took me in as part of your family. You became the family I never had. The birthdays, the picnics and just sitting on the porch talking. You were my family. Alice got up and hugged her mom and dad.

Jim and Sheila, you should be proud of the daughter you have raised. She saved the soul of an angry old man.

I love you both. Alice, I hope the car is as cool as you had hoped. You were my joy. I love you, Goodbye.

The lawyer folded the letter and gave Alice's dad a copy. He said, "The funds will be deposited in the bank of our choice within the week." They all shook his hand and left his office quietly, still not believing what had just happened.

That night the Jamesons sat down to figure out what to do with the money. What would they do with 4.6 million dollars?

Here's what the Jamesons did. They paid off the house and Jim bought a new truck and a small shop to start his own construction company. Sheila paid off all the credit cards, bought a new car, and opened a craft store downtown, like she had always wanted. Neither would have to work again, but these were things they had always wanted to do, but never had the money.

Alice gave up her scholarship to another deserving student and paid her own way to college. She also paid Sara's, Jordan's and Chelsea's college tuition to the college of their choice. The girls and their parents were overjoyed.

Alice and her parents decided that the best way to use the money was to help people. Most of the money went to buying a building, refitting it and opening a retirement home for elderly people. Alice remembered how Mr. Smith said she had saved him, just by being a friend. So, she wanted to try to help more elderly people find friendship and feel wanted. With the help of the Mayor, they were able to begin the process.

After her college graduation, Alice came back and used her Communications degree to recruit area high school students to adopt an elderly person. The student would spend a couple of hours a week with their person. It was kind of like the Big Brother and Big Sister program, but in reverse. Instead of finding adults for kids, they were trying find kids to help adults.

The elderly men and women enjoyed having young people to talk to and being paid attention to. If the pairing worked like it did for Alice and Mr. Smith, both people benefited.

The grand opening was so special for Alice, because Mr. Smith had not wanted the park named after him. She found a way to name the retirement home in his honor anyway. When Alice pulled the sheet from the sign out front, she said, "We dedicate this center as, The Cane Retirement Home!" Everyone cheered.

Jordan, Chelsea and Sara, Alice's best friends, let go of a huge group of helium balloons. As the people started to go into the building, Alice stayed behind with her dad and watched the balloons. She tried to imagine, how Mr. Henry Thadeous Smith would feel about all this.

She glanced up at the balloons as they floated over the building, going higher and higher into the sky. Just for a second, Alice thought she saw the balloons form the shape of a smile as they floated away.

Now, she knew.

THE END

CPSIA information can be obtained
at www.ICGtesting.com
Printed in the USA
LVHW021517290520
656947LV00002B/376

9 781631 293641